Trouble Will Find You

Joan M. Lexau

Illustrated by Michael Chesworth

Houghton Mifflin Company
Boston 1994

Library of Congress Cataloging-in-Publication Data

Lexau, Joan M.
  Trouble will find you / Joan M. Lexau: illustrated by Michael
Chesworth.
    p.   cm.
  Summary: When his parents promise that he can get a puppy if he
can stay out of trouble for just one day, Desmond "Diz" Aster tries
his best, but a burglar almost spoils his efforts.
  ISBN 0-395-64380-5
  [1. Dogs—Fiction.   2. Criminals—Fiction.]   I. Chesworth,
Michael, ill.   II. Title
PZ7.L5895Tp   1994   93-6813
[Fic]—dc20   CIP
                          AC

Printed in the United States of America

HOR   10   9   8   7   6   5   4   3   2   1

for Kevin Alter
with love from
G A Joan

Today Desmond Aster had a plan.

He'd ask a couple of other questions first. Then he'd sneak up on THE question. Maybe then they'd answer it.

"How come we never have pizza for breakfast?" he asked. He put a spoonful of cereal in his mouth. His eyes opened wide in surprise.

"This new cereal is a better way to start the day, Desmond. No sugar. Lots of fiber," his mother told him.

He chewed the fiber. There was lots of it, all right. And no sugar. He started to get up.

"I'll put some honey on it," he said.

"No," his father said. "Honey is sugar, Diz. Eat this stuff the way it is." His father made a face as he chewed the fiber.

Diz was glad his father called him Diz. His friends did, too. He liked it better than Desmond. Diz Aster. His father always said disaster was a good name for him.

His little sister Megan laughed. She slapped her cereal with her spoon. No one yelled at her. Mrs. Aster smiled. She wiped the milk off the table.

"Pepper would buy pizza for breakfast. If they had the money," Diz said.

His father said, "You and Megan follow our rules here. At Pepper's, you follow her mother's rules."

"Me!" shouted Megan. She waved her arms. Her spoon fell on the floor.

Mr. Aster smiled as he picked it up.

Time for the second question.

"Mom, how come you don't stay home all day? Pepper's mother does." Diz licked his spoon to pretend he liked the cereal.

"Don't you like it at Mrs. Rooney's? Isn't she nice to you?" his mother asked. She frowned.

"Did you and Pepper have a big fight?" his father asked.

Diz said, "I like Mrs. Rooney. Pepper is O.K., but she's bossy."

His mother laughed. "Don't scare us like that. It's

so hard to find a good sitter."

"Just stand up to Pepper, son. But don't start a fight," his father said.

Sure, Diz thought. Stand up to her but don't fight! Pepper gets mad easy.

"I have to work," Mrs. Aster said. "Our new house isn't paid for like their old one. That takes more money than one person makes."

"But she does lots of jobs from home," Diz said.

His father said, "Too bad they don't make lots of money. That's why she takes care of you and Megan. She isn't still selling shoes door to door?"

"No. She's making big cookies. To sell at the flea market," Diz said.

"Good," his father said. "Now I can buy my shoes at a store again. Don't tell her I asked about them."

Diz took a deep breath. Time for the BIG question.

"When can I have a dog?" he asked. He looked quickly from his mother to his father.

His mother picked up the paper. She looked at the front page. "It says it will be sunny all day," she said.

This time Diz spoke a little louder. "When can I have a dog?"

His father picked up the other part of the paper. "Oh-oh!" he said. "That housebreaker is still around. In the daytime yet."

Diz wanted to ask how someone could break a house. But not now. "When can I have a dog?" he asked even louder.

Megan coughed a little cough.

"Did you swallow too much milk, Megan?" Mr. Aster asked at once.

"I hope Megan isn't coming down with something," Mrs. Aster said.

Megan smiled. She said, "Me!" and put her thumb in her mouth.

Her mother and father smiled back at her.

"WHEN CAN I HAVE A DOG?" Diz screamed. "WHY WON'T YOU TELL ME?"

Warm, wet tears slid down his cheeks.

· 2 ·

They all stared at Diz.

"But you ask that every day," his mother said.

"We've been over it and over it. You're not ready for a dog," his father said.

Diz closed his hands into two fists.

His father waved his spoon at the window.

"Look at that," he said. "You mother's poor little peach tree."

Only one side had branches.

Diz whispered, "Pepper's trees don't break. I climb them."

His father leaned over to hear him. "Pepper has big strong old trees. This was a little weak tree. Didn't you think about that?" his father asked.

Diz looked away. He didn't know the tree would

break. Or he wouldn't have climbed it. Why couldn't they see that?

His father went on. "What about the frog? The one you put in the Gumbles' swimming pool?"

They never let him forget about that frog. They laughed when they told other people about it. But not when they talked to him.

Diz looked up at his father. "I didn't think you'd want it in the bathtub. I thought it would be happy in a pool."

"Wasn't it happy at the pond?" his mother asked gently.

"I didn't know!" Diz yelled. "How could I know it was going to have babies!"

Diz wiped the tears off his face with his T-shirt.

His mother put an arm around him. "Your father isn't scolding you," she said. "Come on, let's clear the table."

Diz took his bowl to the dishwasher. He was surprised the bowl was empty. The cereal wasn't so bad. It just wasn't good.

His mother looked at his father. "Maybe a dog would keep him out of trouble," she said.

"Ha!" said his father. "First Mr. Gumble calls. Says he saw Diz put the frog in."

"But then I took it out," Diz said. "I didn't see any eggs."

Mr. Aster said, "Then weeks later. All that time we spent. Catching tadpoles with kitchen strainers. We had to empty their pool anyway. And pay to have it filled. The Gumbles still aren't speaking to us."

He turned on the dishwasher and shouted over the clanking. "Tell you what, Diz. Stay out of trouble one day. Just one day. Then you can have a dog."

"Oh, WOW!" Diz yelled.

He pranced around the room. It would be so easy! He'd stay inside at the Rooney's. All day. He wouldn't do a thing. Except think about what kind of dog to get.

"Nothing broken," his father said.

Diz smiled. He wouldn't touch things that break.

"No angry calls from neighbors," his father added. "And no sulking if it doesn't work out."

But it would work out. Diz just knew it!

His father said, "Don't rush into things. Just stop and think. Think about what you want to do. Think about what will happen if you do it."

"O.K.," Diz said. How soon could they go to the dog pound? Maybe tomorrow, he thought.

His mother picked up the paper. "I'll read your fortune, Desmond. This could be your lucky day."

"That stuff is silly," Mr. Aster said.

"I know. But it's fun," she said.

"Let's see. It says I should watch how much I spend. I'll do that. Here's yours, Desmond. Oh!" she said.

Quickly she handed the paper to Mr. Aster. She picked up her purse. "Let's go," she said.

Mr. Aster looked at the paper. He started to cough. He put the paper under his arm. They rushed to the door.

"Hurry, Diz. Take Megan's hand," his father said.

"But what's my fortune?" Diz asked.

"No time," his father said. "Don't want to be late for work."

There was time, Diz thought. How long would it take to tell him? What didn't they want him to know?

· 3 ·

Never mind the fortune. A dog of his own! That was all Diz cared about.

He crossed the street holding Megan's hand. His mother and father drove off. Their blue car turned the corner. It was a sunny day. The kind of day a person could stay out of trouble in.

He took giant steps. Megan laughed. She ran to keep up. Tall rose bushes hid the next front yard. Soon they would be at Pepper's. Safe inside. Away from trouble.

A puppy shot out of the bushes. Diz almost fell over it. The puppy had a lady's pink sock in its mouth.

A man yelled from the other side of the bushes. "Come back with that sock!" he said.

The puppy ran down the street. Diz ran after it.
He picked it up. He cut his thumb. Something sharp
was in the sock.

"Gimme that dog! I'll break its neck!" the man
yelled.

An arm came out of the bushes. Diz saw an eagle tattoo on it. The arm held a long metal bar.

"Ouch!" the man said. "These darn thorns!"

An eye looked at Diz through the bushes.

"Hey, kid," the man said. "Hand that dog over. Or you're in big trouble."

Trouble!

Diz couldn't have trouble. Not today! Or he couldn't have a dog. Would his father make such a deal again?

Diz had a sick feeling in his stomach.

This man wanted to hurt the puppy. Diz had to stop him. That would bring trouble. Diz just knew it!

He hugged the puppy. The puppy licked his face.

"Oh, puppy," Diz whispered. "You don't know how much I want a dog like you!"

He had to stop and think. Not rush into anything. Like his father said. His father made it sound so easy. And it was so hard.

"Push the dog through the bushes. NOW!" the man said.

· *4* ·

Only one thing to do, Diz thought. Even if it got him in trouble.

"No," Diz said. "Not if you're going to hurt it. I don't care if it is your dog. I'll . . . I'll call the police."

The man said quickly, "It isn't mine. Just hand over the sock. You can keep the dog." The eye still stared at Diz.

Just for a second, Diz was so happy. He could keep this dog!

No. It had to belong to someone.

But Diz could get his own dog. If he could only stay out of trouble.

O.K. Just give the sock to the man.

Diz put the puppy down and tried to pull the sock away.

"Ouch!" Diz said. Something sharp cut him again.

He moved his hands away from the sharp thing. It was a game to the puppy. The more Diz pulled, the more the puppy pulled.

"Hurry up!" the man said. "Get the sock. Or toss the dog over here. I'll get the sock away, all right."

"Please, puppy," Diz whispered. His voice was shaking. "Please let go of the sock."

"I'll come get the dog now," the man said.

A woman's voice said, "Do you think you should?"

Diz heard the man say, "Ruby." That must be the lady's name, he thought. There was more talking. He couldn't hear it clearly.

A voice came from down the street. "Diz! Megan! Why are you standing there?"

It was bossy Pepper. She could never mind her own beeswax. She was standing by her house.

Diz heard the lady say, "That does it. Let's get out of here."

Diz heard a lot of banging and crashing.

"Leave the TV," the man said. "It's broken."

"I forgot," the woman said.

Diz heard car doors slam.

At last the puppy let go of the sock.

A van shot out of the driveway. An old green van.

The tires squealed. It drove down the street away from Diz.

Diz waved the sock at it. He yelled, "Hey! Your sock!" He started to run down the street. Megan ran after him. "Megan, get out of the street!" he shouted. She stood there with her thumb in her mouth. Diz pulled her back to the sidewalk.

The van turned the corner. It was gone.

Diz looked down. The puppy wagged its skinny tail. The dog had long, floppy ears. Its legs were short and fat.

"Do you live in this house?" Diz asked. He took the dog to the driveway. Diz gave the dog a push. The dog would not move.

"You must live around here," Diz said. "Go home, dog."

The big round eyes looked at Diz. The puppy looked like it was asking a question.

"It's O.K.," Diz said. "I'll find out where you live." Maybe Pepper would know.

Diz picked up the puppy. "Come on, Megan," he said. They went to Pepper's house. She was waiting for them.

Pepper said, "You got a dog! That's great, Diz."

"It isn't mine," Diz said.

Pepper put her hands on her hips. "Now what have you done?" she asked. That was just like Pepper.

Diz told her about the man. He showed her the sock. There was blood on it now. "There's something sharp inside. It cut me," he said.

Diz turned the sock upside down. He gave it a shake. Something fell on the grass. He picked it up.

"It's pretty," Pepper said.

Diz pushed his glasses up to see better. They were always down his nose. His father said Diz yanked them off. That's why they were loose.

It was a lady's gold pin. There was a red stone in it.

"Wow!" Diz said. "That's why the man wanted the sock. Maybe this cost a lot."

If it did, he was in big trouble!

· 5 ·

"Let's ask your mother what to do," Diz said.

They went into Pepper's house. It was a big old house. It had a big yard. Diz liked it better than his own.

Only Pepper and her mother lived here. Pepper's father lived far away. He sent her a letter at Christmas. Or on her birthday.

Mrs. Rooney was making cookies. They made the house smell good.

"Mother," Pepper began. "Diz has someone's pin. And someone's dog." She sure knew how to make it sound bad.

"Let me tell it!" Diz yelled. He told Mrs. Rooney about the puppy. And the mean man. "I couldn't let him hurt the puppy," Diz said.

"I know," Mrs. Rooney said. "What did he look like?"

Diz said, "There was a lady named Ruby, too. But I didn't see them." He showed her the sock and the pin.

Mrs. Rooney looked at the pin. "I don't think it cost so much. Not if they drove off and left it."

"So Diz can just keep it. Right?" Pepper asked.

"No," her mother said. "He can take it back later. Someone just moved there. A woman, I think. I don't know if her name is Ruby. No big deal, Diz."

"That's good," Diz said. "I have to stay out of trouble all day. If I do, I can have a dog."

"I'm so glad," Mrs. Rooney said. "I know how much you want one."

"I don't know, Diz," Pepper said. "You stay out of trouble? But I'll help you. Don't I always?"

Diz put the pin in the sock. He put the sock in his pocket. Pepper thought bossing him was helping him. But she was a good friend, Diz thought.

Mrs. Rooney said, "A puppy can stray pretty far. Why not put some signs up? Maybe the owner will see one."

"Neat," Pepper said. "We'll put them on poles. I'll get the crayons and paper. And some tacks."

Pepper also found a box for the puppy. "To keep it out of trouble in the house," she said.

Diz and Pepper sat on the floor to make signs.

Pepper pushed her red hair away from her eyes. Her hair always fell over her face. Her real name was Piper. Piper Rooney sounded like pepperoni. She liked being called Pepper. But hated people saying her hair was cute.

Megan helped make signs. Hers were all scribbles.

I FOUND A PUPPY, Diz put on the paper. CALL ME UP.

"Do I put my phone number on it? Or yours?" he asked Mrs. Rooney.

"Put our number on it," Mrs. Rooney said. "I'd better go make more cookies now. The flea market is tomorrow."

"You have to charge a lot of money for them. All that butter and stuff. They cost a lot," Pepper said.

Pepper is even bossy to her mother, Diz thought.

"I'll make lots of cookies," her mother said. "Then I'll make more money." She went to the kitchen.

Pepper sighed. "She'll sell them real cheap. So more people will buy them. And she'll lose money. She always does," she told Diz.

Diz thought, Pepper's mother never worries. But

Pepper seems to worry all the time.

Pepper looked at his sign. "No, no, no!" she said. "Not like that." She showed him her sign. It said:

FOUND
on Spring street
Black and White
PUPPY
Big long ears
please call 829-

Diz wished he could say his sign was better. But hers was better. He made three signs like Pepper's.

The puppy got out of its box. It picked up a sign in its teeth. Soon the sign was all little bits of paper.

Megan laughed. She gave the puppy a hug.

"Bad dog," Pepper yelled.

The puppy hung its head. It put its tail between its legs.

Diz put the puppy back in the box. He patted it

on the head. The puppy licked Diz's hand.

"The puppy doesn't know any better. Don't yell at it," he told Pepper.

"You have to teach a dog. Yelling teaches it," Pepper said.

Diz didn't want to start a fight. Maybe Pepper was right. He made a new sign.

"Well, let's go put them up," Pepper said.

Diz didn't want to go out. But he had to. He hoped he could stay out of trouble. Somehow.

Pepper put Yellow in her backpack. Yellow was her big old stuffed cat. When it was new it was yellow. Now it was sort of gray. Pepper took Yellow everywhere with her. She put the signs and tacks in also.

"Give me that pin, Diz. You lose things," Pepper said.

Diz started to say no. But he did lose things. Pepper never did. He handed her the sock.

"I don't want that dirty sock," Pepper said.

Diz took the pin out and gave it to Pepper. He stuffed the sock back in his pocket. The lady would want her sock back, too.

Pepper pinned the pin on Yellow. She shut the backpack.

Diz saw a newspaper on a chair.

"Wait," he said. "I have to see my fortune." He found the page. He looked for July, his birthday month.

"Oh, no! It can't be!" Diz yelled. But there it was. TROUBLE WILL FIND YOU IF YOU LET IT.

· *6* ·

"I'm not going!" Diz shouted. He stood with his back against the door. He shoved the newspaper at Pepper. "Look at my fortune," he said.

Pepper read his fortune. She laughed.

"Mother!" Pepper called. "Diz is scared of his fortune."

Mrs. Rooney came in and read it. She didn't laugh. But she smiled. "It's just silly," she told Diz. "Someone made it up."

Pepper said, "They didn't know you have to stay out of trouble today."

Diz thought about it. His mother and father said it was silly, too. But they didn't let him see it.

"Then why is it there today? Why not some other day?" Diz asked.

Mrs. Rooney said, "It happens. My mother had to take a plane one day. Her fortune said to keep your feet on the ground."

"Did she take the plane?" Diz asked.

"Of course," said Mrs. Rooney. "She had a good trip."

Diz took a deep breath. Maybe it will still be O.K., he thought.

Mrs. Pepper said, "It's nearly noon. Better eat before you go."

They went to the kitchen. Pepper made peanut butter sandwiches. They ate them and then they each ate a big cookie.

"Boy, is this good!" Diz told Mrs. Rooney.

"There's a little beef stew left," Pepper's mother said. She took it out and gave it to the dog. The dog ate it in big bites.

"Take the dog with you," Mrs. Rooney said. She found a rope for it.

Diz tied one end around the puppy's neck. He put his fingers under it. "That isn't too tight," he told the dog. The puppy wagged its tail.

Diz and Pepper went out the back door. They went down the alley.

"We'll put a sign on the corner," Pepper said.

"Let's stop at that house," Diz said.

He hoped that man wasn't back. But he wanted to return the pin and sock. Then they wouldn't get him in trouble.

They came to the backyard of the house. Diz and Pepper both stopped.

"What a mess!" Pepper said.

A TV was on the grass. A big clock was near it.

Diz found a broken glass jar. There were pennies all around it.

"Look. Here's a toaster," Pepper said.

Diz picked up a long metal bar. "That man had this thing," Diz told Pepper. "I think he was going to hit the puppy with it."

Diz found a pile of socks.

A watch was in one. The others were empty.

"Let's go see if someone is home," Diz said.

The back door was standing open.

Diz yelled, "Hello! Is anyone home?"

They waited. It was very quiet. "Why is this stuff all over the yard?" Pepper whispered.

Diz whispered back. "Your mother said the lady just moved in. Maybe the man was helping her move more stuff."

"Then why did they leave such a mess?" Pepper asked.

Diz was thinking the same thing. The man and lady left so fast. As if they were scared. Scared of what? Maybe they were crooks. Maybe they were taking stuff away, not bringing stuff here. Maybe they left too fast to take it all.

He didn't want to say it. Pepper might laugh at him. He'd have to think it over.

"I don't like it," Pepper whispered. "Let's come back later."

That was fine with Diz.

They ran all the way to the corner. The puppy had a hard time keeping up.

"Your legs are too short," Diz told the dog.

"We'll put a sign on that pole," Pepper said.

But the pole already had a sign.

"Wow!" Diz said. "The dog's owner put up a sign. This is the strayed puppy, all right."

He told the puppy, "We found your home. It's O.K. now."

So why did Diz feel so bad? He sighed. "O.K., let's take the dog home," he said.

Pepper looked at him.

"I'm sorry, Diz," she said. "But you'll get a real good dog. Just as good as this one."

Diz looked away. He didn't want to think about it. He just wanted to get it over with.

It was not far to 21 Maple Street. Just six blocks away. On the way, a van went slowly by them. An old green van.

Diz saw the driver's arm. It had a tattoo of an eagle. A lady sat next to him.

"I think that's the man," Diz told Pepper. "He has the same tattoo. That looks like the van."

The driver looked at Diz. The van roared away.

Pepper said, "They acted scared of us!"

Diz thought, They must be crooks! He would ask Mrs. Rooney about it later.

Twenty-one Maple Street was a small blue house. Diz knocked on the door.

A woman opened the door.

Diz gave the puppy a quick hug.

"Goodbye, puppy," he whispered. He hoped he wasn't going to cry. He stood up.

The woman said, "Oh, good! You saw my sign about the dog I found. Here is your puppy back."

She handed a black and white puppy to Diz.

The woman shut the door.

· 7 ·

Diz had a hard time holding the new puppy. It wiggled and wiggled. He had to set it down.

The two puppies ran round and round each other. The puppy on the rope went round and round Diz. His legs were tied up. He fell down.

"Take it easy!" he yelled.

He grabbed one dog. It was the new puppy. Its tail was long and fluffy. It had longer legs than the first puppy. But they looked a lot alike.

Pepper rang the doorbell. She knocked on the door. She pounded on the door.

At last the door opened.

"What do you want?" the woman asked.

A little radio was around her neck. She took earphones off of her ears.

"That isn't our puppy," Diz said. He was still on the ground.

The woman looked down at him.

"Sure it isn't," she said. "It looks just like your other puppy. You can't dump them here."

She looked at Pepper. "I like your red hair, kid. It's cute."

SLAM went the door.

Pepper said, "She makes me so mad, I could spit!"

Diz untied the first puppy. The two dogs ran around like crazy. Diz pulled the rope off his legs. He stood up.

Diz and Pepper pounded on the door. No one came.

They looked in the window next to the door. The woman was pushing a vacuum cleaner. The ear-phones were over her ears. Her hips were wiggling.

Pepper said, "She can't hear us."

"She sure walks funny," Diz said.

Pepper said, "She's dancing to the radio, Diz!"

"Oh," said Diz.

The woman turned and saw them. She frowned and turned her back.

Pepper said, "We could just leave them. Why do we have to find where they live?"

"No!" Diz said. "They might run in the street. They could get run over."

"I know," Pepper said. She sighed. "We better go home. We have to make new signs. Signs that say two puppies."

Diz grabbed a dog. It was the new puppy. He tied the rope on it.

"Let's go down the alley," Diz said. "Then that puppy can't run in the street."

But the first puppy ran all around them. It was hard not to fall over it.

"You carry that puppy," Diz told Pepper.

"No," Pepper said. "It will wee-wee on me. Dogs wee-wee all over. Cats wee-wee in boxes. Cats are smarter."

"You don't know a thing about dogs!" Diz yelled. "Dogs come when you call them. They do what you want. Cats only do what cats want. Cats are dumb!"

Pepper stopped walking. She faced Diz.

"That shows how smart cats are!" she yelled. "Dogs can't think on their own. Cats are . . ."

She stopped yelling.

"Boy, if I didn't have to take care of you," she said.

"Take care of me!" Diz yelled. "I'm older than you! Two months older."

"Then act like it!" Pepper snapped. "Why are you always in trouble?"

Diz was about to yell some more. But he remembered what his father said. Don't start a fight with Pepper.

They looked at each other.

Pepper said, "I can't fight with you."

"Why not?" Diz asked.

"My mother said not to," Pepper said. "We need the job taking care of Megan."

Diz started laughing. He couldn't help it.

"What?" Pepper asked.

"I can't fight with you," Diz said. "We need your mother to take care of Megan."

Pepper grinned. "Isn't it crazy?" she said.

Pepper took the rope out of Diz's hand. He picked up the other puppy. He held the puppy close. The puppy licked his chin.

"Don't get to liking me," Diz whispered. "I can't keep you."

They started walking again.

Ahead of them Diz saw an old green van. It was parked in the alley.

The mean man was walking to the van. He was carrying a TV set. Now Diz was sure the man was a crook.

"Look!" Diz told Pepper. "That crook is stealing a TV."

"Let's go around that house. Don't let him see us," Pepper said.

In front of the house, Diz bumped into a woman. She was taking letters out of her mailbox.

"A man is stealing your TV," Diz told her. "He's in the alley."

"That's really funny!" the woman said. "Come with me."

She led them around the house.

Diz saw the crook putting the TV in the van.

"Young man, wait," the woman said. "You want to hear something funny?"

The crook looked at Diz. It was not a nice look.

The woman said, "This little boy told me you stole our TV."

The man laughed. "The things a dumb kid will say!"

He shut the van door and turned.

The front of his T-shirt said

    There was a picture of a TV. It had a sad face on it.

    "Oh, Diz!" Pepper said. "You see how you get in trouble?"

· 8 ·

The woman told Diz, "My TV broke. So I called Stan's shop. They will fix it at the shop."

The man said, "You can't go around calling people crooks!"

"I'm sorry," Diz said. He hung his head.

"I should tell your folks," the man said.

Diz looked up at the man. "I didn't mean to . . . I just thought . . ."

The man said, "But I won't. Just watch it next time!"

He winked at the woman.

She smiled and went into her house.

SLAM went the back door of the van. The man got in front. Ruby sat next to him. The man rolled down the window.

"Why are you kids after us? Leave us alone. Or you'll be sorry!" he said.

"But we're not . . ." Diz began.

The van drove off.

Diz sighed. So the man was not a crook.

He felt very mixed up. All he'd tried to do was to help. First the puppy. Then the lady with the TV.

"How will you ever get a dog this way?" Pepper said. "Come on. Let's go home."

They walked back to the sidewalk.

Diz looked at the puppy in his arms. Its tongue was hanging out. It was panting in quick little pants. The other dog was, too.

"It's hot," Diz said. "The dogs need water."

"We have water at home," Pepper said.

They walked to the next block. Diz looked across the street. He saw a man with a hose. He was watering his grass.

"Let's ask that man," Diz said.

"Oh, all right," Pepper said.

They crossed the street.

Diz heard a dog yip. It was not one of the dogs with them. The dog Diz held wiggled out of his arms.

"I think it has to wee-wee," Diz said.

But the puppy took off. It ran in back of a house. The dog with Pepper tried to pull away. She held on to the rope.

"Puppy, come back here!" Diz yelled.

"Look at that," Diz told Pepper. "See? It comes when I call. I told you dogs are smart."

"Smarter than some people," Pepper said. "That isn't the same puppy, Diz."

Diz looked again. This puppy was brown and white. Not black and white. One more puppy ran after it. This one was almost all brown.

Then the black and white puppy came back.

The man with the hose was next door.

"Are these two dogs yours, Mister?" Diz asked.

"No," the man said. "I saw four puppies dumped this morning. Some creep in a red car. Tossed them out and drove away."

He added, "Two puppies stayed here. Your two look like the others."

Oh, no! Diz thought. He had to find new homes for the two dogs he had.

"Can our puppies have some water? They're hot," Diz said.

"Why not?" the man said.

Diz made a cup out of his hands. All four puppies

wanted to drink. They pushed each other away.

"Are you going to keep your two? Or take them to the pound?" Diz asked the man. Maybe the man would take all four, he thought.

"It isn't my problem," the man said. "I have a dog. And the pound has too many now. People should have their dogs fixed. Then they couldn't make puppies."

He rolled up the hose.

"You want these two? I'll fix some ropes," the man said.

"O.K.," Diz said. He didn't look at Pepper.

"I know, I know," she said. "You can't leave them on their own."

The man cut three more ropes. Diz took two dogs. Pepper took two dogs.

They walked down the block. At the corner was a drug store. They crossed the street.

Pepper said, "You know what? You have a lot of dogs. For a kid who can't have a dog."

"You mean WE do," Diz said.

"You found the first one. You started it. And Yellow doesn't like dogs," Pepper said.

Diz said, "Yellow is stuffed. How could she like dogs?"

"Yellow is better than a real dog. Some day I'm going to have a real cat. But I'll still keep Yellow," Pepper said.

The dogs pulled this way and that. Soon the four ropes were tangled up.

Diz stopped. He looked up at the sky. "How can I find homes for all these dogs?" he wailed.

· *9* ·

Diz tried to untwist the ropes.

"Can't do it," he said. "We have to untie the dogs."

Pepper helped him.

"We can make new signs," Diz said. "*Homes Wanted* signs."

"O.K.," Pepper said. "If no one calls, your dad can take them to the pound."

"Yes," Diz agreed sadly.

The dogs were free of the ropes. Three dogs ran off. Diz picked up the one that stayed. It was the dog he'd saved from that mean man. Diz ran one way. Pepper ran the other way.

Pepper grabbed a puppy. She tied a rope to it.

Diz chased a puppy in back of a house.

"Oops!" he said. He ran into a lady. He saw it was Ruby.

The mean man came out of the back door. A computer was in his arms. He had a sock on each hand. His mouth fell open. He almost dropped the computer.

He must fix computers, too, thought Diz. Now he could give back the pin and sock.

"We have your red pin," Diz said.

"It's a trick," the man told Ruby. "See if the cops are out front."

Ruby left. She came back.

"No cops," she said. "Just the other kid."

Pepper and a puppy were with her. Pepper put a rope on the puppy Diz just found.

Cops! Diz thought. He's afraid of cops. They are crooks!

"You kids get lost. And stay lost this time," Ruby said.

"Don't tell the cops on us. They won't believe you," the man said. "You told that woman down the street. She laughed at you."

"Let's go," Diz told Pepper. He turned to run.

"Look. In his pocket," Ruby said.

Diz looked at his pocket. The pink sock was hanging out.

He ran. The man and woman ran after him.

Diz found the last puppy. He tripped over it. He fell to one side to miss the puppy. His glasses fell off. His knee landed on them. The frame broke with a snap.

"You O.K.?" Diz asked the puppy in his arms.

"Yip!" said the puppy. It sounded O.K.

The man came up to Diz. He grabbed the sock.

"I've got it!" he told Ruby.

"Don't tell the cops about this," he told Diz. "Or I'll say you took it. I took it back to return it."

Diz thought, He must be crazy about socks!

The man looked inside the sock.

Diz started to get up. The man stood over him. His face was red with anger.

"I've had too much from you kids. Where is that ruby?" he said.

Diz was getting really scared. He pointed at Ruby. "She's over there."

"Doris doesn't have it," the man snapped. "Where is the ruby? The red pin?"

"Oh!" Diz said. "I don't have it."

He looked at Pepper. She dropped the ropes. She started to run away. She pushed her hair off her face so she could see where she was going.

She's taking off. She's leaving me! Diz thought.

Pepper took Yellow out of her backpack. She waved the stuffed cat.

"The pin is on my cat," she yelled.

The man and Doris ran after her. They went down the alley.

Pepper will die if they get Yellow! Diz thought.

He yelled, "Pepper! Take the pin off Yellow. Throw it to them."

Pepper yelled back, "Get away from there, Diz."

Diz knew she was making them run after her. So he could get away. He grabbed two ropes. He picked up the other two dogs. There was just time to hide behind a lilac bush.

The man and woman came back.

"That girl sure can run," Doris said.

"Just find the boy. We'll make him get the ruby," the man said. "I'm not taking any more nonsense from these kids."

They looked all over.

"I don't see him," Doris said.

"Yip," said a puppy. "Yap," said another puppy. "Yip yip yap yip," said all the puppies.

"Behind that bush," the man said.

Diz ran. He pulled two puppies on ropes. He had a puppy in each arm. He ran to the front of the house. The man and woman ran after him.

Diz remembered something his mother told him. If you get scared of somebody, yell. Yell things like, Somebody help me! Or, Let me be, you're not my dad!

He opened his mouth to yell. He looked across the street. A man was in front of the drug store. He was getting into a car. Diz had an idea.

"Dad!" Diz yelled. "Wait for me!"

Diz only saw his back. But he knew it wasn't his father. He didn't care. He ran to the car.

· 10 ·

Diz looked back across the street. He saw the man and Doris run in back of the house. A motor started. They were gone.

Diz took a deep breath. He turned and looked up. Into the face of Mr. Gumble.

Mr. Gumble with the swimming pool. The pool Diz put a frog in. The frog that had tadpoles. The tadpoles that Diz and his mother and father worked so hard to get out. With kitchen strainers.

Mr. Gumble scowled.

"Young man, I am NOT your father," Mr. Gumble said. "Thank heaven for THAT! And get those dogs away from me."

Diz pulled the puppies away. Could he explain to Mr. Gumble? About two crooks and a ruby and four

puppies with no homes? No. "Sorry," he said.

"You always are," Mr. Gumble said. He got in his car and drove away.

Diz sighed. "Come on, dogs," he said. "We have to find my glasses." He went back to where he fell. Pepper was there, holding his glasses.

"You can tape them," she said. "I'll help you." She put them in her backpack.

"Mom and Dad will see the tape," Diz said. "Dad will say I'm not ready for a dog. Even if they don't find out about the ruby."

"You couldn't help it, Diz," Pepper said. "You were right about that man. But you'll have a dog some day. Just like I'll have a cat."

It was the first time Pepper ever said he was right. About anything.

"Thanks," he said.

Diz tied up the loose puppies. They each took two ropes. They walked slowly home. Now and then they stopped. The ropes kept getting tangled.

Diz kept an eye out for the van. They were nearly at Pepper's house.

"Here's where I found the first puppy," Diz said.

They looked down the driveway. A gray car was in it. A woman was looking at the mess on the grass. She picked up a sock and dropped it.

"She must live here," Diz told Pepper. "Let's give her the ruby."

Diz couldn't wait to get rid of it. They could tell her about the crook. She could call the police.

Diz and Pepper wouldn't have to worry about it any more.

The woman saw them. She came over.

"Children, did you see . . ." she began.

She saw the ruby pin in Pepper's hand. The woman grabbed it.

"You two wait right here," she snapped. "I'll tell the police you broke into my house."

"But . . ." said Diz.

"Don't try to run away," the woman said. "I know you live around here. The police will find you."

"But . . ." said Diz.

The woman didn't wait. She ran into her house.

Pepper wailed, "She thinks I'm a crook! Just because I tried to help you!"

Diz looked away. Now even Pepper was mad at him.

His fortune was right. Trouble had found him, all right. "If you let it," the paper had said.

How did he let it?

· *11* ·

They waited for the police to come. The woman watched them from the driveway. The dogs ran round and round.

"We'll just explain to the police," Diz said. "Then it will be over."

"I hope so," Pepper said.

Diz hoped so, too.

A police car came. Two police officers got out.

The policeman said, "I'm Sergeant Hawkins. This is Officer Wicks."

"I'm Ms. Zimmer," said the woman who lived in the house.

"And you kids?" said Officer Wicks, a policewoman.

Pepper said, "I'm Pepper Rooney. This is Diz Aster."

"Say what?" said Sergeant Hawkins.

"Desmond," said Diz.

"Oh!" the sergeant said.

The woman said, "They broke into my house. Took my ruby pin. They threw these things all over."

"We didn't —" Diz began.

"I'm not a crook," Pepper said.

"When did this happen?" the sergeant asked.

He took out a notebook.

"We didn't . . ." Diz began again.

"I never . . ." Pepper began.

The woman said, "I don't know. I just got home from work."

"Did they take anything else?" asked the police-woman.

"But we didn't . . ." Diz said.

"I wouldn't . . ." Pepper said.

The woman said, "I didn't look yet."

Diz had had it. He stood in front of the sergeant. He yelled, "WHY WON'T YOU LISTEN TO US!"

The sergeant looked down at Diz. He put his hands on his hips.

"Well?" he asked.

Pepper said, "Diz found a puppy. That was the

first thing."

"SHUT UP, PEPPER!" Diz yelled. "You weren't there then."

Pepper's mouth fell open.

Diz thought, She likes being bossy. But not being bossed.

Diz explained about the dogs and the crooks. And the ruby. No one else said a word. Even Pepper. She looked hurt. That made him feel bad.

Diz told how Pepper made the crooks run after her. So he could get away from them.

Pepper grinned. "I can run fast," she said.

"Smart!" said Officer Wicks. "But if you have to run, drop everything. Don't carry anything. Then you can run faster."

The sergeant said, "They wanted the ruby. So you should throw it one way. Then you run the other way. And then call us. Or tell your parents. Or someone you know."

The policewoman said, "We tell kids to run, yell, and tell. Nobody has a right to tell you not to tell. Not if they hurt or scare you."

"Nobody," said the sergeant. "Even if they make you say you won't tell. O.K.?"

Diz and Pepper nodded.

Ms. Zimmer said, "Come to think of it . . . These kids didn't act as if they had done something wrong. I'm sorry, Diz and Pepper. I was so upset."

"That's O.K.," Diz said. He felt much better now.

"So what did this man look like?" the sergeant asked.

Diz said, "He was tall and skinny. Not very old. He looked mean."

"A lot of people look like that," said Officer Wicks.

"And his name is Stan," Diz said. "I saw it on his T-shirt. Stan the TV Man."

"Good work," said the sergeant.

"I know that shop," Ms. Zimmer said. "I called them about my broken TV. It's on Highland Road."

"I have to find homes for all these puppies," Diz said.

"They are cute," Ms. Zimmer said.

Diz got an idea.

"You could use a watchdog," he told her.

She laughed. "You're right." She picked out the brown dog.

Officer Wicks said, "My little girl has a birthday next week. She's been asking for a dog." She picked out a black and white dog. The one with the fluffy tail.

Only two dogs left, Diz thought. He had the first dog he found. And the brown and white one.

The sergeant said, "We'll get your parents, kids. Then we'll go see Stan the TV Man."

Diz did not want to face his parents. But there was no help for it.

The police picked up Mrs. Rooney and Megan. Mrs. Rooney called Diz's parents at work. They said they would meet them at Stan's TV shop. Ms. Zimmer went in her car.

On the way, Diz and Pepper told Mrs. Rooney about the crooks. Diz felt really good. Now it was almost over.

There was a man inside the shop. He had gray hair. He was fat. He was short.

The sergeant said, "We want to see Stan."

"I'm Stan," said the man with gray hair.

The police looked at Diz.

· 12 ·

Diz said, "But his T-shirt said *Stan* on it."

"What T-shirt?" Stan asked.

"The crook's T-shirt," Diz said. "The man with the eagle tattoo."

"That's my new helper," Stan said. "What is this about?"

Diz told the story again. He added something he had left out before.

"That man likes socks. He even wears them on his hands," Diz said.

The two police officers spoke at the same time. "The Sock Burglar!"

"Fingerprints," Officer Wicks said. "He wears socks so he won't leave any."

"And he puts rings and old coins and stuff in

socks. He dumps any extra socks when he leaves," the sergeant said.

"I was glad to have a new helper. He even used his own van. But so slow!" Stan said. "I thought he was lazy."

"He was housebreaking. And fixing TVs, too," the sergeant said.

"Breaking houses?" Diz asked.

"Breaking into houses," Officer Wicks said. "With a prybar. We didn't know about the woman. Ruby," she added with a grin.

Diz said, "He had a long metal bar. He was going to hit the puppy with it."

"That's the prybar," said the sergeant.

"It's funny," Ms. Zimmer said. "I called here yesterday. About my broken TV. Today that man breaks into my house."

"You didn't talk to me," Stan said.

"Are you sure?" Ms. Zimmer asked. "I said to come on Saturday. I work on weekdays. Oh!"

"You talked to my helper," Stan said.

The sergeant said, "Yes. You told him when you aren't home. So that's when he broke in."

The sergeant looked at Stan's book. It showed where TVs were fixed.

"A lot of these homes were broken into. By the Sock Burglars," the sergeant said.

"Your helper is a crook," Diz told Stan. "I think you need a watchdog."

Stan smiled. "I'd like a dog to talk to. While I work," he said. "What about that black and white one? His eyes look like he's always asking a question."

"Oh," said Diz. That was the first puppy he found. The one he liked best. He wanted it to have a really good home. Someone he knew.

But Stan seemed nice.

Diz picked up the puppy and hugged it. He felt the tears in his eyes.

"It's O.K.," Stan told him. "That other one is fine too."

Stan picked up the other puppy.

Just then the crook walked in. He was carrying a TV. He took one look and turned and ran.

Officer Wicks grabbed him.

"No, you don't," she said.

"You going to listen to those kids?" the crook said.

The sergeant said, "I'll look for the van. See if that woman is in it."

He came back with Doris.

"It was Matt's idea," Doris said. "I just rode along."

Matt yelled, "No, you don't! You were in it all the way! You wanted that ruby."

Diz's mother and father rushed in.

"Diz didn't mean to do it! What did he do?" his father yelled.

Officer Wicks said, "He got the Sock Burglars for us."

Ms. Zimmer said, "He found homes for three puppies."

Pepper said, "He just wanted to help a puppy. Then things went wrong. You know how it is with Diz."

Megan went over to Diz. She held his hand.

Diz told it all again. He was tired of talking about it.

His parents didn't say a word. They just looked at him.

Diz looked down. "I know our deal is off," he said. "I got in trouble. And I broke my glasses."

He looked at the puppy in his arms.

"I have to find a home for this puppy. Do you know a really good home?" he asked.

"I sure do," his father said.

Diz whispered in the puppy's ear. "You'll have a nice home," he said. His voice shook.

His father said, "With a boy who can take care of four puppies. And catch crooks at the same time. With Pepper's help."

Diz looked up. "Huh?" he said.

"We said you weren't ready for a dog. We were wrong," his mother said.

"A puppy needed help," his father said. "It could mean trouble. You might not get your own dog. But you helped."

"We're proud of you, Desmond!" his mother said.

Diz told Pepper, "My fortune was wrong. I'm not in trouble. And I have a dog of my own now."

Pepper said, "That's great, Diz. Call it Patches. It has black and white patches."

"I'LL NAME MY OWN DOG!" Diz yelled.

He looked at the puppy. "Trouble didn't find me. You found me," he said.

Diz laughed. "I'll make the fortune come true. I'll call the dog Trouble."

Trouble licked Diz on the nose. Then it shut its eyes. The puppy fell asleep in his arms.

It was a long full day for a little puppy.

Diz wanted to yell and run. He was so happy.

But he looked down at Trouble. And he sighed with joy.